This book

....

....

....

Retold by Gaby Goldsack
Illustrated by Emma Lake (Advocate)
Designed by Jester Designs

Language consultant: Betty Root

ISBN 1-84461-310-0

Marks and Spencer p.l.c.
PO Box 3339
Chester, CH99 9QS
www.marksandspencer.com

Copyright © Exclusive Editions 2002

Printed in China

The Enormous Turnip

Helping Your Child to Read

Learning to read is an exciting challenge for most children. From a very early age, sharing story books with children, talking about the pictures and guessing what might happen next are all very important parts of the reading experience.

Sharing reading

Set aside a regular quiet time to share reading with younger children, or to be on hand to encourage older children as they develop into independent readers.

First Readers are intended to encourage and support the early stages of learning to read. They present well-loved tales that children will happily listen to again and again. Familiarity helps children to identify some of the words and phrases.

When you feel your child is ready to move on a little, encourage them to join in so that you read the story aloud together. Always pause to talk about the pictures. The easy-to-read speech bubbles in **First Readers** provide an excellent 'joining-in' activity. The bright, clear illustrations and matching text will help children to understand the story.

Building confidence

In time, children will want to read *to* you. When this happens, be patient and give continual praise. They may not read all the words correctly, but children's substitutions are often very good guesses.

The repetition in each book is particularly helpful for building confidence. If your child cannot read a particular word, go back to the beginning of the sentence and read it together so the meaning is not lost. Most importantly, do not continue if your child is tired or simply in need of a change.

Reading alone

The next step is for your child to read alone. Try to be on hand to give help and support. Remember to give lots of encouragement and praise.

Together with other simple stories, **First Readers** will ensure that children will find reading an enjoyable and rewarding experience.

Once upon a time an old man and an old woman lived in a little cottage. One day, the old man planted some turnip seeds.

Every day, the old man watered the turnip seeds. Soon tiny leaves started to grow.

The old man was pleased. The turnips grew bigger and bigger.

Soon, one turnip was bigger than
the rest.

It kept on growing.

It grew bigger...

...and bigger...

until, one day, it was enormous!

The old man was very pleased.

One day, the old woman decided to cook the enormous turnip.

The old man tried to pull it up.
He pulled and he pulled. But he
could not pull it up.

He called to the old
woman to help him.

So the old man pulled the turnip, and the old woman pulled the old man.

They pulled and they pulled. But they could not pull it up.

The old woman called to the boy to help.

17

So the old man pulled the turnip, and the old woman pulled the old man, and the boy pulled the old woman.

They pulled and they pulled.
But they could not pull it up.

The boy called to the girl to help.

So the old man pulled the turnip, and
the old woman pulled the old man,
and the boy pulled the old woman,
and the girl pulled the boy.

They pulled and they pulled.
But they could not pull it up.

Then the girl called to the donkey
to help.

So the old man pulled the turnip, and
the old woman pulled the old man,
and the boy pulled the old woman,
and the girl pulled the boy, and the
donkey pulled the girl.

One last try.

They pulled and they pulled. But they could not pull it up.

The donkey called to the goat to help.

So the old man pulled the turnip, and
the old woman pulled the old man, and
the boy pulled the old woman, and
the girl pulled the boy, and the donkey
pulled the girl, and the goat pulled
the donkey.

Pop!

They pulled and they pulled. Then, pop! The enormous turnip came flying out of the ground. Everyone fell down.

It really was the most enormous turnip they had ever seen. The old woman cooked the turnip.

Everyone thought the turnip soup
was very tasty. Donkey and goat
thought so too.

The old man was very pleased
with himself.

Read and Say

How many of these words can you say?
The pictures will help you. Look back in
your book and see if you can find the
words in the story.

cottage

boy

girl

donkey

goat

leaves

man

soup

turnip

woman

Titles in this series,
subject to availability:

Beauty and the Beast
Chicken-Licken
Cinderella
The Elves and the Shoemaker
The Emperor's New Clothes
The Enormous Turnip
The Gingerbread Man
Goldilocks and the Three Bears
Hansel and Gretel
Jack and the Beanstalk
Joseph's Coat of Many Colours
Little Red Riding Hood
Noah's Ark and other Bible Stories
Rapunzel
Rumpelstiltskin
Sleeping Beauty
Snow White and the Seven Dwarfs
The Three Billy Goats Gruff
The Three Little Pigs
The Ugly Duckling